Happy Cat First Readers

When Anna Slept Over

Anna's going to stay at Josie's house. She's excited, but worried too. Sheepy, her tattered old piece of rug, helps her sleep. Will everyone laugh at her? And will she get to sleep at all?

Happy Cat First Readers

When Anna Slept Over

Jane Godwin

Illustrated by
Andrew McLean

HAPPY CAT BOOKS

For my dear little niece, Ella. *J.G*

Published by
Happy Cat Books
An imprint of Catnip Publishing Ltd
14 Greville Street
London EC1N 8SD

First published by Penguin Books, Australia, 2001

This edition first published 2011
3 5 7 9 10 8 6 4 2

Text copyright © Jane Godwin, 2001
Illustrations copyright © Andrew McLean, 2001

A CIP catalogue record for this book is available
from the British Library

ISBN 978-1-905117-25-3

Printed in India

www.catnippublishing.co.uk

Chapter One

Anna's mum and dad were going to a wedding in the country.

'We will be gone for a day and a night,' said Mum.

'Can I stay with Nanna and Grandpa?' asked Anna.

'Nanna and Grandpa are

going to the wedding as
well,' said Mum.

'Can I stay with Auntie
Liz and Uncle Mark?' asked
Anna.

'They will be at the
wedding, too,' said Mum.

'Well,' said Anna, 'who
can I stay with?'

'Would you like to stay

with Josie?' asked Mum.

'Stay at Josie's place all night?' said Anna.

'Yes,' said Mum. 'Would you like to do that?'

'Yes!' said Anna. 'I'd love to do that!'

Chapter Two

Josie was Anna's friend
at school. They had played
at each others' houses. They
had even stayed for dinner.
But they had never stayed
the night.

'We can have fish and
chips for dinner,' Josie told

Anna the next day. 'And we
can watch a video and stay
up till ten o'clock. Mum
said we could. And we
can have pancakes for
breakfast. I can't wait!'

Anna was excited about
the sleepover. But thinking
about breakfast at someone
else's house made her feel
not quite sure.

'Why can't I come to the
wedding?' Anna asked her
mum after school. 'I went
to Auntie Liz's wedding.
I was the flower girl. Can't
I come?'

'Some weddings are just

for the adults,' said Mum.
'Anyway, you'll have a
lovely time at Josie's.'

'But everyone is going to
this wedding,' said Anna.

'You and Dad. Nanna and Grandpa. Auntie Liz and Uncle Mark. Everyone except me.'

As bedtime drew closer, Anna felt a bit cross about the wedding and the sleepover and everything.

Dad came in to kiss her goodnight. Anna was snuggled down in bed with her old bit of sheepskin rug. She had been given the rug

when she was a baby. Now
there was just a little bit
left. She held it against her
face when she went to sleep.
She used to call it Sheepy.
Sometimes she still called
it Sheepy, even though she
was in Grade One.

'Look at old Sheepy,'
said Dad. 'There's not much
of Sheepy left, is there?'

'There's enough left,'
said Anna. She rubbed

10

Sheepy between her
fingers.

Suddenly, a thought
struck her. Josie didn't
know about Sheepy. Josie
wouldn't have a Sheepy,
Anna was sure of it.

Josie would think bits of
old blanket were only for
babies.

'What will I do about
Sheepy?' she asked Dad.

'What do you mean?' said
Dad.

'Tomorrow night! What
will I do? I don't want Josie
to see Sheepy!'

'Why not? Josie might
have a special toy to take
to bed, too.'

'But not like Sheepy. Not
a baby's thing. I can't sleep
without Sheepy. And Josie's

14

brother might see. He'd laugh at me.' Anna sat up in bed and started to cry.

'I'm sure Josie would understand,' said Dad. 'She's a good friend.

She wouldn't laugh at you.'

'But she might tell someone at school,' sobbed Anna. 'And then people would tease me!'

'Would you like to leave

Sheepy at home for the night?' asked Dad.

'No!' said Anna. 'Then I could *never* get to sleep!'

'Can you take a teddy instead?' asked Dad.

'A teddy's not the same as Sheepy, Dad,' said Anna.

Dad sat on the edge of Anna's bed. He thought for a moment.

Then he had an idea.

Chapter Three

The next morning, Dad
picked up Anna's pillow.
Into the pillowcase, right
down the bottom, they put
Sheepy.

'That way,' said Dad,
'when you're in bed, you
can sneak Sheepy out in

the dark and no one will
know. Then in the morning
you can pop Sheepy back in
the pillowcase.'

Anna stood the pillow gently by the front door.

Soon it was time to go to Josie's.

'What happens if I need you in the night?' asked Anna.

'You can phone us to say goodnight if you want to,' said Mum. 'Would that make you feel better?'

'Yes,' said Anna.

'And you've got Sheepy in your pillowcase,' said Dad.

'Don't tell Josie's mum about Sheepy,' said Anna.

'Okay,' said Mum. 'I won't.'

Chapter Four

When they got there, Josie
ran up to the car.

'I'll take your pillow!'
she said.

'NO!' said Anna. 'You can
take my backpack if you
like.'

Anna followed Josie

inside. She laid the pillow
carefully on the folding bed.

Mum stayed for a cup of
tea.

Josie and Anna jumped
on Josie's trampoline. Josie
had a big dog called Billy.
He barked and sometimes
he jumped up and put his
paws on the trampoline.

'Get down, Billy!' shouted
Josie's brother, Sam.

Josie let Anna jump first.
Anna was going up and
down, up and down. Billy
kept barking.

Anna started to feel sick.

'You can have a go now,'
she said to Josie. Anna went
inside and sat with Mum
while she finished her cup
of tea.

'It's time for me to go,'
said Mum.

She gave Anna a hug.
'See you tomorrow, darling.'

Anna clung on to Mum.
'Goodbye, Mum,' she
whispered. 'I might ring
you up later.'

Josie's mum took Anna's
hand. 'Let's go outside and
see what Josie is doing.'

Anna looked back at
Mum. Mum looked back
at Anna. They waved. Then
Mum was gone.

Chapter Five

In the afternoon, they went
to the park. Anna and Josie
played on the monkey bars.
'Look at me!' called Josie.
'Can you do this?'

Mum and Dad would be
in the car now, driving to
the country, Anna thought

as she went down the slide.

I wonder if they'll be there yet, she thought as she sat on the swing.

Josie's dad bought three ice-creams from the ice-cream man. Billy kept trying to get licks of them.

Josie threw Billy his old tennis ball. He ran back with it. He stood there with his tail wagging.

'Drop,' said Josie firmly. 'Drop, Billy.'

Billy dropped the ball.

'Do you want to throw it?' Josie asked Anna.

Anna took the ball. It was warm and wet and slimy. She threw it. Billy leapt up and caught it in the air.

'Drop!' said Josie, when
Billy ran back. 'Drop, Billy.'

Chapter Six

When they got home it was
bath time. Josie's mum
filled it up with blue bubble
bath.

Josie's dad went to get
the fish and chips.

Sam ate his really
quickly. 'Have you finished

with your chips, Anna?' he
asked.

'No,' said Anna. 'I've only
had one.'

Josie's mum and dad
laughed.

'Sam just wants to eat
yours,' said Josie.

'Your mum and dad would
be at the wedding now,' said
Josie's mum. 'Would you like
to ring them up?'

'Not yet,' said Anna. 'I'll ring them later.' She felt grown-up and brave. It was fun, sleeping over. She ate her hot, salty chips and smiled at Josie.

After dinner, Josie's dad gave them each a chocolate frog. Sam swallowed his in one gulp.

'Let's not eat ours yet,' whispered Josie. 'Let's save them.'

'Yes!' said Anna. 'Let's put them in your room for later.'

Josie giggled.

Sam put the video on.

'Would you like to bring your pillows out here and lie on the couch?' asked Josie's mum.

Sam jumped up. 'I'll get
them!' he said. He came
back, dragging three pillows.

Oh, no, thought Anna.
She grabbed her pillow
and felt around inside.

She peered down into the
pillowcase. She pushed
the pillow from one side to
the other, looking all around.
Where was Sheepy?

Chapter Seven

'What's wrong, Anna?'
asked Josie's mum.

'Um,' said Anna. 'Um . . .'

She ran down the
hallway into Josie's room.
She looked under the
folding bed. She looked
under the quilt.

Where was Sheepy?

'Anna!' called Josie. 'What are you doing?'

Anna's heart was beating fast. She had to find Sheepy!

Just then, Billy walked past the bedroom. He had something in his mouth.

Anna ran after him into the living room.

'What's Billy got?' said Sam.

They all looked.

It was Sheepy.

Chapter Eight

Billy was a big, slobbery
dog. Anna had always been
a bit scared of him. She
looked at Sheepy in Billy's
mouth. She could see his
spit on Sheepy.

'Drop,' she said quietly, just
like she'd seen Josie do. 'Drop.'

Billy looked up. His big
eyes were red and sad-looking.

Anna looked back at him, sternly. 'Drop.'

He dropped Sheepy at her feet.

Anna grabbed Sheepy and shoved it back in her pillowcase.

'What's that?' asked Josie. 'What did he have in his mouth?'

'It looked all dirty and yukky,' said Sam.

'It was just something from my pillowcase,' said Anna. 'Some old thing that I don't need any more.'

'Who wants some popcorn while you watch the film?' asked Josie's mum.

'Me!' shouted Josie.

'Me!' shouted Sam. So Anna shouted 'Me!' as well.

After the video, it was time for bed.

'Do you want one of Josie's teddies to keep you company?' Josie's mum asked Anna.

Anna chose a little brown one. She tucked the teddy into bed next to her.

'It's time to turn the light off now,' said Josie's mum.

They lay in bed. They talked and giggled and talked again. They ate the chocolate frogs in the dark.

Josie's mum came back. 'No more noise, okay?'

Chapter Nine

It was dark. Josie was
asleep. Anna lay in the
folding bed. The sheet was
tight. The little teddy
beside her felt new and
scratchy.

Now I can get Sheepy
out, thought Anna.

But what would happen
if Josie woke up and saw
Sheepy beside Anna? Anna
lay for a while on her back.

'Mum and Dad!' she
suddenly remembered.
'I never rang up Mum
and Dad!' She sat up.

'Josie,' she whispered.
'Josie, I need to ring up
Mum and Dad. I need to
say goodnight to them.'

But Josie was sound
asleep.

Anna sat on the edge
of the bed. She felt hot
and worried. She crept out

of bed and down the
hallway to Josie's parents'
bedroom. Would they be
cross with her?

'What's wrong, Anna?'
asked Josie's mum.

'I need to ring up Mum
and Dad,' she said. 'I need
to say goodnight to them.'

'It's very late. Can you ring them in the morning?' asked Josie's dad.

'No, I need to say goodnight to them. They said I could ring,' said Anna.

'Okay, let's go and phone them.'

Anna rang her dad's mobile number.

When it answered there was lots of noise. 'Hang on!' she heard him say.

Then it was quieter.

'Hello?' said Dad.

'Dad, it's me!' said Anna.

'Anna! What are you doing up? It's a quarter to eleven!'

'I just rang to say goodnight.'

'Oh,' said Dad. 'Well, goodnight, Anna. And go to sleep!'

'Can I speak to Mum?'

'Hang on. I'll get her.'

'Hello, darling.' It was so lovely to hear Mum's voice. 'Isn't it time you were asleep?'

'Yes,' said Anna. 'I'm just saying goodnight to you and Dad.'

'Okay. Well, goodnight, and see you tomorrow at lunch time. Off you go to bed.'

'Goodnight, Mum,' said Anna.

Anna hung up.

'Everything all right?' asked Josie's mum.

'Yes,' said Anna.

She skipped back to
Josie's room.
'Goodnight!'

Chapter Ten

When Anna woke up the next morning, she suddenly remembered where she was. And then she remembered something else. Sheepy!

She hadn't taken Sheepy out of the pillowcase. She had gone to sleep without Sheepy!

After breakfast, Anna
and Josie bounced on the
trampoline. They rode on
the bikes. They talked to
Josie's friends next door.
Then Mum and Dad came
to pick her up.

'Can I stay for a bit longer?' asked Anna. 'Please?'

Chapter Eleven

That night, Anna went to
bed early.

'Was everything okay with
Sheepy last night?' Dad
asked.

'I didn't need Sheepy.
I didn't even get Sheepy out
of the pillowcase,' said Anna.

'That was very grown-up
of you,' said Dad.

'But I think I'll have
Sheepy tonight,' said Anna.
She held Sheepy against her
face.

Dad kissed Anna goodnight.

Anna lay down in her
very own bed.

She thought for a little
while.

She had been on a
sleepover.

She had stayed at Josie's
all night.

She had thrown the ball
to Billy.

And she had even gone
to sleep without Sheepy.

She felt very happy.

From Jane Godwin

Once I stayed overnight at a
friend's beach house. My mum
stayed for the day and my friend
and I built a boat in the sand.
I kept looking at my mum and
thinking, 'Soon she'll be going home
and I'll be staying here.' I felt
happy and sad at the same time.
Sometimes sleepovers are like
that, I think.

Do you think so too?

From Andrew McLean

I know exactly how Anna felt when she visited Josie. When I was a child I went to stay at a farm in Orbost. I was supposed to stay there for a few days, and was really looking forward to riding a horse for the first time. After only one day at the farm, I became so homesick that I had to go home. Luckily, I don't get homesick any more.

The Princess and the Unicorn

Wendy Blaxland

No one believes in unicorns any more. Except Princess Lily, that is.
So when the king falls ill and the only thing that can cure him is
the magic of a unicorn, it's up to her to find one.
But can Lily find a magical unicorn in time?

THE LITTLEST PIRATE

SHERRYL CLARK

Nicholas Nosh is the littlest pirate in the world. He's not allowed to go to sea. 'You're too small,' said his dad. But when the fierce pirate Captain Red Beard kidnaps his family, Nicholas sets sail to rescue them!

Nobody is better at being bad than Buster Reed – he flicks
paint, says rude words to girls, sticks chewing gum under
the seats and wears the same socks for weeks at a time.
Naturally no one wants to know him. But Buster has a
secret – he would like a friend to play with.
How will he ever manage to find one?

The Magic Wand

Ursula Dubosarsky

Becky was cross with her little brother. 'If you don't leave me alone,' she said to him, 'I'll put a spell on you!' But she didn't mean to make him disappear!

The Gorilla Suit

Victor Kelleher

Tom was given a gorilla suit for his birthday. He loved it and wore it everywhere. When mum and dad took him to the zoo he wouldn't wear his ordinary clothes. But isn't it asking for trouble to go to the zoo dressed as a gorilla?

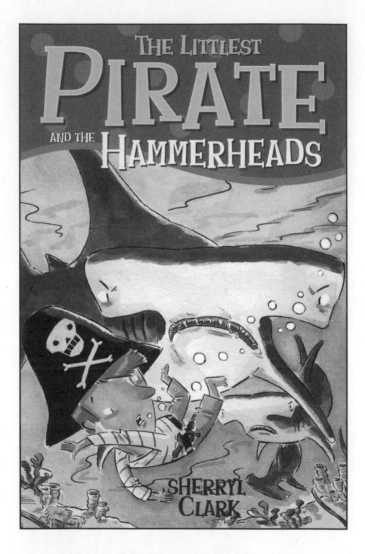

Nicholas Nosh, the littlest pirate in the world, has to rescue his family's treasure which has been stolen by Captain Hammerhead. But how can he outwit the sharks that are guarding Captain Hammerhead's ship?

THE MERMAID'S TAIL

RAEWYN CAISLEY

Crystal longs to be a mermaid.
Her mother makes her a flashing silver tail. But it isn't like
being a proper mermaid. Then one night Crystal wears her
tail to bed...